Big Dog and Little Dog go Sailing

☆ Selina Young ☆

Blue Bananas

Other titles in the bunch:

Big Dog and Little Dog Go Sailing
Big Dog and Little Dog Visit the Moon
Colin and the Curly Claw
Dexter's Journey
Follow the Swallow
"Here I Am!" said Smedley

Horrible Haircut
Magic Lemonade
The Magnificent Mummies
Midnight in Memphis
Peg
Shoot!

Crabtree Publishing Company
www.crabtreebooks.com

PMB 16A, 350 Fifth Avenue
Suite 3308
New York, NY 10118

612 Welland Avenue
St. Catharines, Ontario
Canada, L2M 5V6

Young, Selina.
    Big Dog and Little Dog Go Sailing / Selina Young;
    p. cm. -- (Blue Bananas)
    Summary: Big Dog and Little Dog's adventures on their new boat
include fishing, water skiing, and exploring a very unusual island.
    ISBN 0-7787-0845-4 -- ISBN 0-7787-0891-8 (pbk.)
    [1. Boats and boating--Fiction. 2. Dogs--Fiction. 3. Whales--
Fiction.] I. Title. II. Series.
PZ7.Y8792 Bi 2002
[E]--dc21

                           2001032445
                                 LC

Published by Crabtree Publishing in 2002
First published in 2000 by Mammoth an imprint of Egmont Children's Books Limited
Text and illustrations copyright © Selina Young 2000
The Author and Illustrator have asserted their moral rights.
Paperback ISBN 0-7787-0891-8 Reinforced Hardcover Binding ISBN 0-7787-0845-4

1 2 3 4 5 6 7 8 9 0 Printed in Italy 0 9 8 7 6 5 4 3 2 1

Big Dog was an inventor.
Some days he invented lots of things
and some days he didn't.

Last Tuesday Little Dog helped
Big Dog make a shiny red boat.
(Just like that!)

Big Dog bounced out of bed extra early

and bounded noisily

down

the

stairs.

Tra la la dum de dee!

Little Dog was still snuggled up in bed when Big Dog burst in with the breakfast tray.

Big Dog ate his breakfast and talked excitedly with his mouth full. Today was the day for trying out their new boat.

Little Dog thought this sounded fun

so she got up and washed behind her

ears and put on a clean scarf.

Big Dog made a list of all the things

they should take with them.

Little Dog packed all the things into a big basket. She put in her umbrella just in case.

Big Dog made his favorite sandwiches, peanut butter, cheese, and jam.

At last they were ready to go.

Big Dog was so excited he raced

out of the door and ran on ahead.

The boat was tied to the dock.

It bobbed up and down in the water.

Big Dog galloped up the gangplank
and leaped on board.

Big Dog and Little Dog's boat
was made out of lots of
bits and pieces. It had:

A motor for calm days.

A sail for windy days.

A wheel for steering.

A lever for going fast or slow.

A telescope for looking through

Big Dog turned the key and the engine started. Chug splutter chug chug. Carefully he steered the boat through the harbor and out to sea.

Then Big Dog pushed the lever to "Fast"
and off they zoomed. Their ears flapped
as they whizzed along. The boat went
thump thump against the waves.

Big Dog thought that going fast was amazing. Little Dog wasn't so sure. She'd rather be fishing.

Big Dog stopped the boat in a shady cove and dropped the anchor with a S P L O S H!

They got out their fishing rods and
Big Dog helped Little Dog put bait
on her hook.

Big Dog and Little Dog threw their
lines out to sea and waited for the fish
to start biting.

It wasn't long before Big Dog felt

a sharp tug. It must be a fish!

He pulled on his line.

It was hard work.

A horrible monster with spikes

came flying out of the water.

The spiky fish pulled itself free and swam away.

"I don't like fishing anymore," said Big Dog. "Let's do something more exciting."

"Like what?" asked Little Dog.

After that they went snorkeling.

Big Dog took a bag to collect shells.

One, two, three, they jumped into the

water with a big splash.

Snorkeling was fun.

Little Dog liked counting the fish.

Big Dog was busy seeing how many

shells he could fit in his bag.

When Big Dog's bag was full of shells, they swam back to the boat for some lunch.

After lunch the sky got darker and a
fierce storm began to blow. Big Dog and
Little Dog went down below to make
some hot chocolate and warm up.

Big Dog was just pouring the milk into the mugs when **Bump!** the boat hit something!

They had crashed into a big island.

Big Dog dropped the anchor and

Little Dog lowered the gangplank.

Little Dog grabbed her umbrella and

Big Dog took his telescope. Then

they ran ashore.

"Let's explore," said Big Dog. Together they ran up the hill to the top of the island. It was very hard work. The ground was so shiny and slippery.

At the top of the island they sat down
and took turns looking through the
telescope.

Then Big Dog felt rain drops.

Plip plop! Big drops of rain began to fall out of the sky. But there was not a rain cloud in sight. Little Dog put up her umbrella. Splish splash went the rain.

Suddenly there was a big rumble and the
island began to shake. It was so bumpy
Big Dog and Little Dog fell over and
tumbled down the hill.

They jumped aboard their boat and hid
under their bunks.

Just then a big voice said, "Whoops!
I've bumped into someone's boat.
I hope I didn't tip them over."

Little Dog peeped out from under the
table and saw a big black eye at the
porthole. A deep voice said, "Hello,
anyone home?"

Big Dog and Little Dog came out from their hiding places but all they could see was the island.

"I'm sorry I bumped you," the voice said kindly. "I always seem to be bumping into something. Last week it was the lighthouse and it hurt my nose."

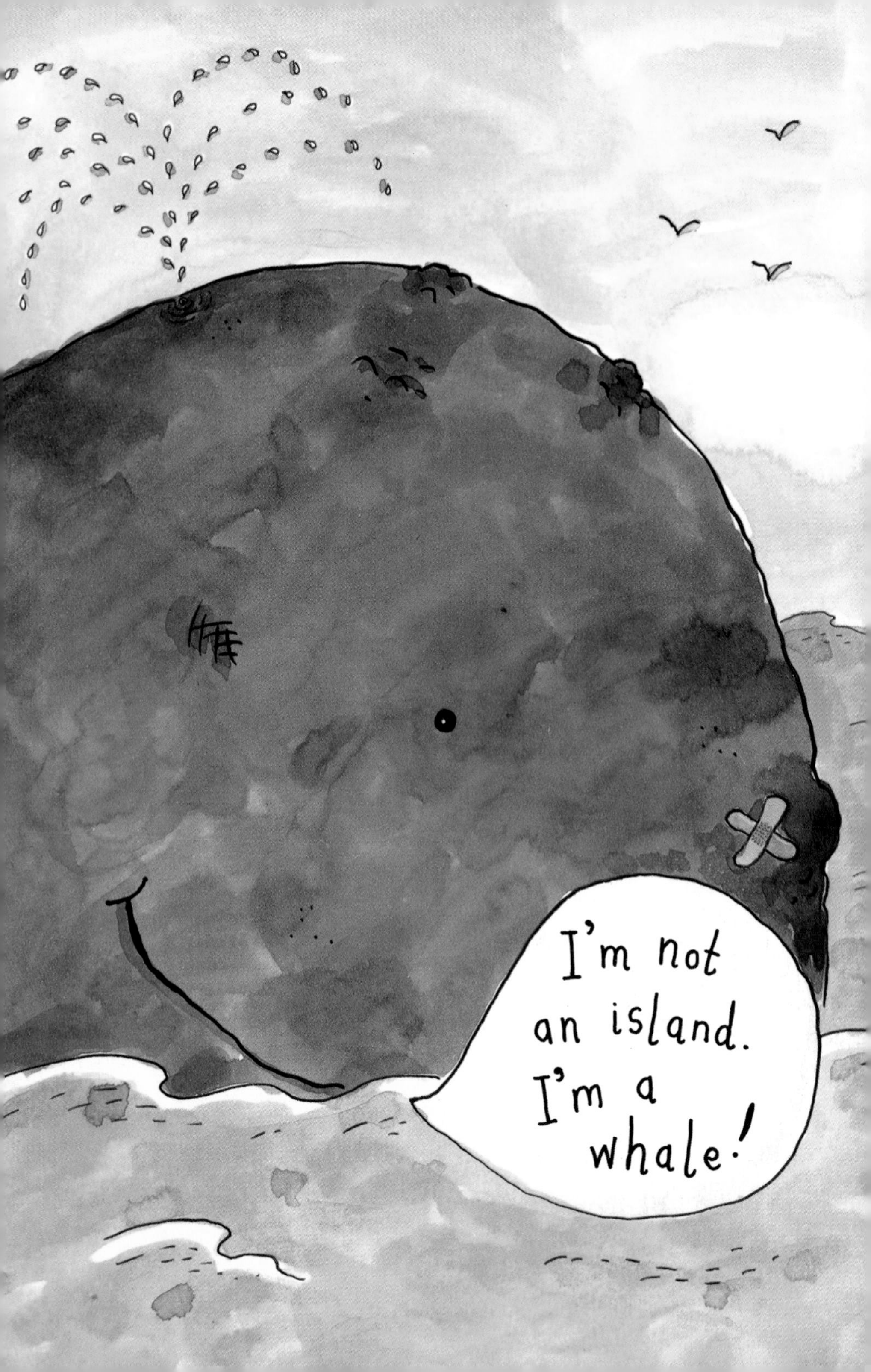
I'm not an island. I'm a whale!

The whale explained how he kept falling asleep and drifting into things. He showed Big Dog and Little Dog all his bumps and bruises.(They were very sympathetic.)

Little Dog suddenly had an idea.

She whispered into Big Dog's ear.

"Good thinking!" said Big Dog. "Whale

can have our anchor!"

Whale thought it was such a great idea
he offered Big Dog and Little Dog
a ride home on his back.

What an exciting boat adventure they had. Little Dog helped Big Dog pull the boat up on the beach. Then they raced home for supper.

Big Dog cooked some fish sticks.

Little Dog mashed some potatoes.

Then it was time for bed.

Little Dog went to sleep right away.

But Big Dog was wide awake planning

a very special adventure for next weekend.